THE BIGGEST FROG IN AUSTRALIA

SUSAN L. ROTH

Simon & Schuster
Books for Young Readers

SIMON & SCHUSTER BOOKS FOR YOUNG READERS
An imprint of Simon & Schuster Children's Publishing Division
1230 Avenue of the Americas, New York, New York 10020.
Copyright © 1996 by Susan L. Roth
All rights reserved including the right of reproduction
in whole or in part in any form.
SIMON & SCHUSTER BOOKS FOR YOUNG READERS
is a trademark of Simon & Schuster.
Book design by Lucille Chomowicz
The text for this book is set in Stone Sans Semibold.
The illustrations are rendered in collage.
Manufactured in the United States of America.
First Edition
10 9 8 7 6 5 4 3

Library of Congress Cataloging-in-Publication Data
Roth, Susan L.
The biggest frog in Australia / written and illustrated
by Susan L. Roth.
p.   cm.
Summary: When a thirsty frog drinks up all the water in
Australia, the other animals must think of a way to make him
give it up.
ISBN 0-689-80490-3
[1. Frogs—Fiction. 2. Australia—Fiction. 3. Tall Tales.] I. Title.
PZ7.R73Bi 1996   [Fic]—dc20 95-9721

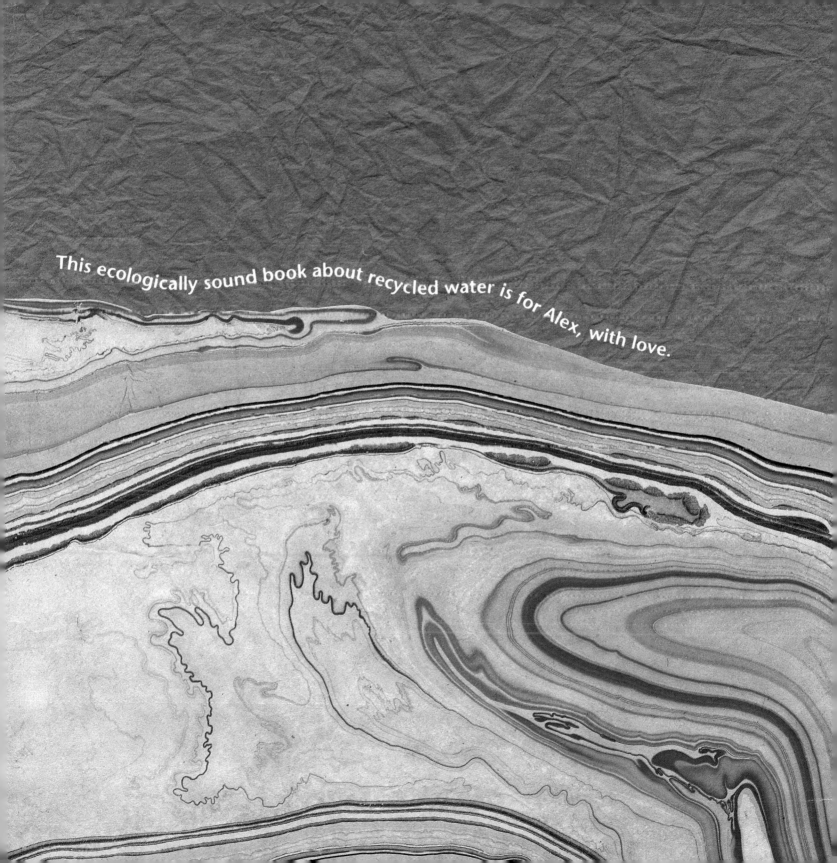

This ecologically sound book about recycled water is for Alex, with love.

Once, in the Dreamtime, the biggest

frog in Australia woke up very thirsty.

He was so thirsty that he drank up all the water in all the puddles.

Then he drank up all the water in all the billabongs. Next he drank up all the water in all the rivers and in all the lakes. But even after all that drinking, he was still thirsty.

The biggest frog in Australia was
so thirsty that he drank up all the
water in the ocean. He jumped
into the sky and drank up all the
water in the rain clouds.

And then, finally, the biggest frog wasn't thirsty anymore.

He sat in the outback, bloated, full to his eyeballs with all the water in Australia.

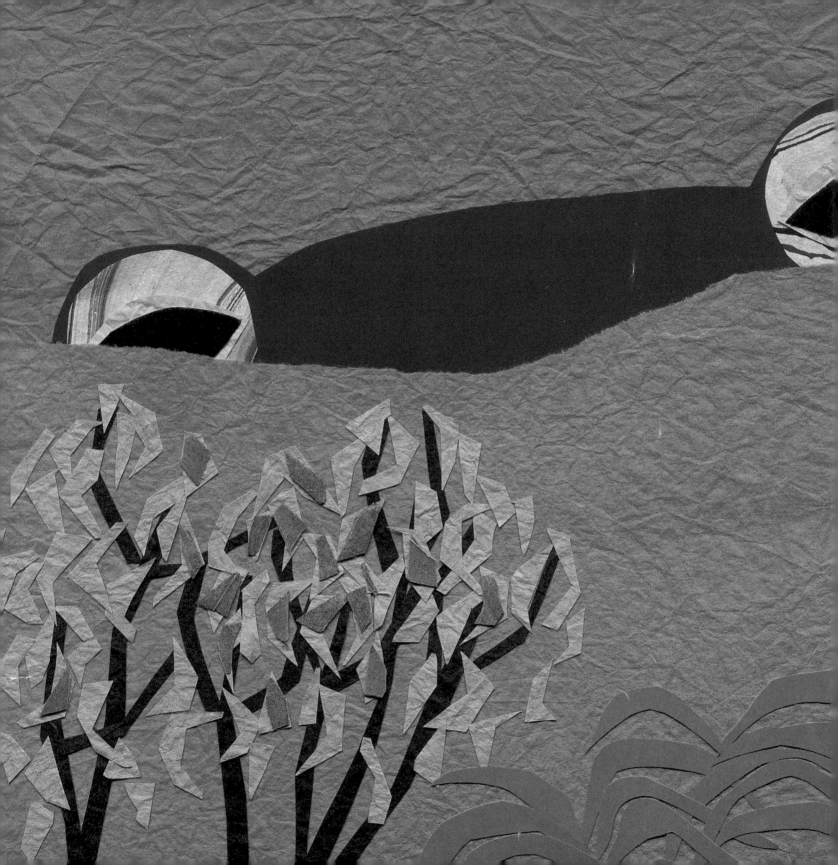

This was fine for the biggest frog. But the earth became dusty. Eucalyptus trees shriveled. Wallaby grasses bent over. Flowering wattles dropped their petals. And then all the rest of the animals were thirsty, because the biggest frog had left them nothing to drink.

One day wise old Wombat spoke
to his friends in a parched voice.

"If we could make the frog laugh, the water would spill out of his mouth and go back to where it belongs."

"I'll start!" screeched Kookaburra. "I've got a good one! Where does the saltwater crocodile lie down when he's tired? Anywhere he wants! Ha-ha-ha!" Kookaburra was laughing so hard at her own joke that she could barely get the words out of her mouth. "Ha-ha-ha!" cackled all the other animals.

But the biggest frog in Australia didn't even smile.

He was too busy thinking about how he wasn't thirsty anymore.

Next was Kangaroo.

First he jumped backward over Platypus. Then he jumped backward over Dingo,

but he jumped too far

and landed upside down in a tree.

All the animals chuckled and clapped.
Except the biggest frog in Australia.
He looked as if he were asleep with his eyes open.

When it was Koala's turn, he waddled up and down on two legs, sticking his belly out as far as it would go. "You look ridiculous!" bellowed Echidna. Koala turned and waddled in the other direction.

He started to wiggle and shake his bottom.

The animals stamped their feet
and shouted with laughter.

They were having such a
good time that they almost
forgot they were thirsty.

But the biggest frog in
Australia didn't even blink.

Only Wombat remembered how thirsty he was. He was furious at the biggest frog.

"Let's tickle him!" he shouted angrily.

Just then the animals noticed the frog move his head.

He was watching two eels
who were
half crazed
from being
out of the water
for so long.
They were
dancing,
slowly at first,
but then faster
and faster.
They twisted
their bodies
into the
silliest
shapes.

Before long, the eels had tied
themselves into a slipknot.
When they tried to move, the
knot only became tighter. They
pulled and *pulled*...

...and finally slipped apart with such force that they rolled up like a spring

and landed on either side of the biggest frog.

By now the animals were too thirsty even to smile.
But there was a flicker in the eyes of the biggest frog in Australia.

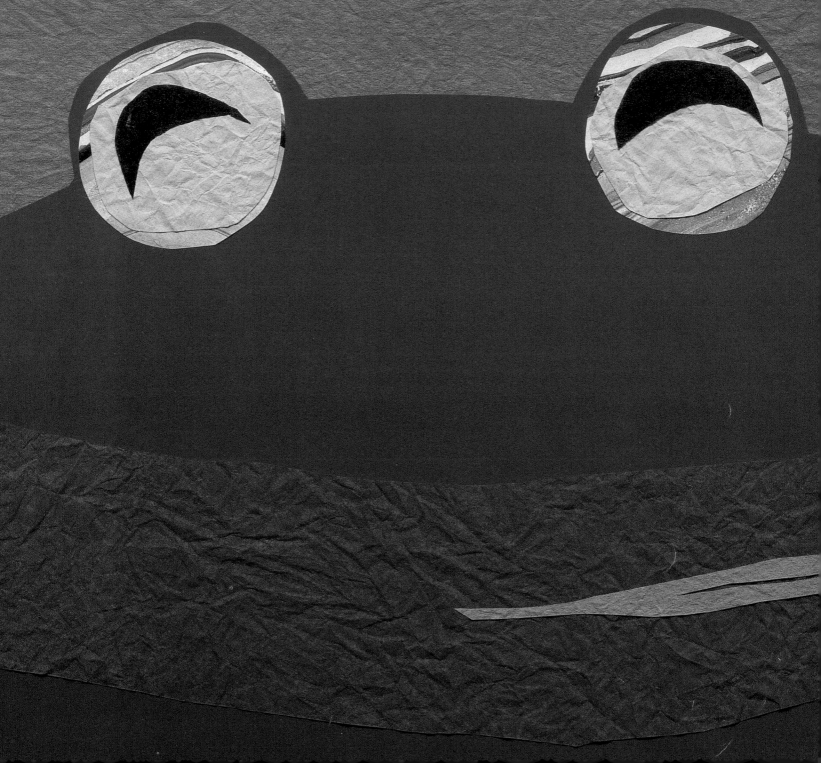

The frog let out a soft giggle, then another.
He snorted and a little water squirted
out of the side of his mouth.

Encouraged,
the eels

then stood
on their heads
and
wrote
their
names
in cursive.

At that,
the biggest
frog in Australia
opened his mouth
and guffawed.

The other animals jumped up and ran for their lives.

They scattered as fast as they could in every direction as the biggest frog laughed out all the water in Australia. He laughed the water back to the clouds in the sky and back to the bottom of the ocean. Into the lakes and the rivers, the billabongs and the puddles.

And once they were safe on high ground,
the other animals laughed along with him.

"Oh, me," croaked the biggest frog in Australia.
"Eels are so silly!"

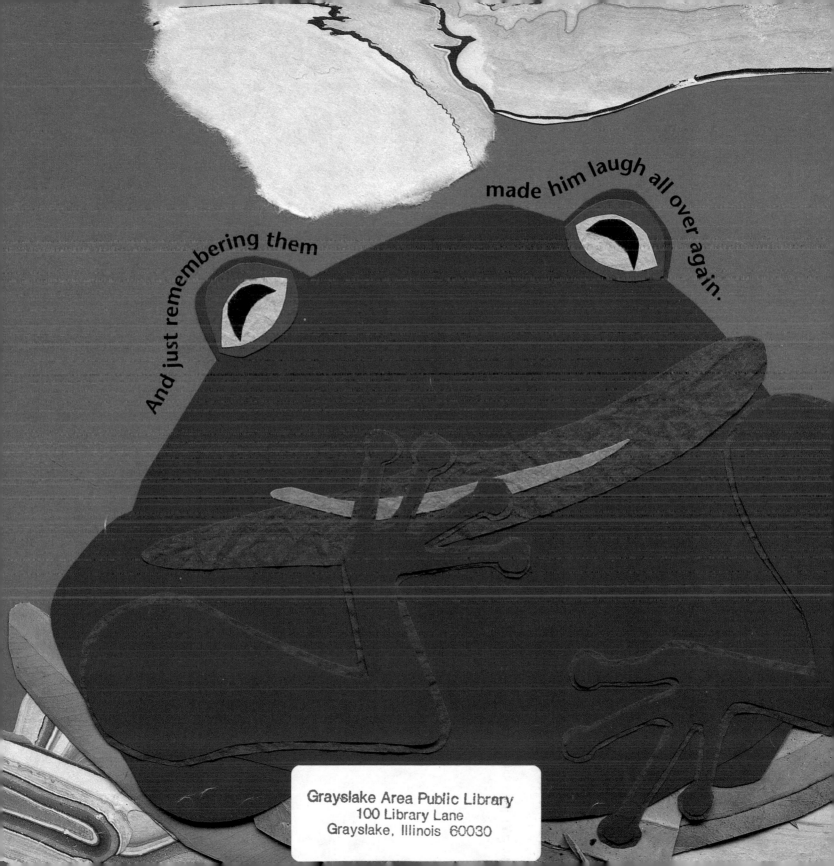

And just remembering them made him laugh all over again.

Glossary and Author's Note

The inspiration for this story came from "Tiddalik the Flood-maker" in *The Dreamtime: Australian Aboriginal Myths in Paintings* by Ainslie Roberts with text by Charles P. Montford (Rigby Ltd., 1976, Adelaide, Australia). I have found different versions of the story in several anthologies; I especially thank Martin Beadle and Nancy Patz for their generous sharing of each of their collections.

The collages are rendered in papers that come from all over the world. They also include real eucalyptus leaves from California trees, but who is to say from where their seeds blew? The collages pay homage to the reddest frog in Australia, which I saw at the Taronga Park Zoo in Sydney; Aboriginal bark paintings; and contemporary, original prints by Australian artists.

S. L. R. *Baltimore, Maryland*

Australian Aboriginals:	The earliest human inhabitants of Australia
billabong:	The Aboriginal word for a branch of a river that flows away from the main stream and ends
dingo:	An Australian wild dog
dreamtime:	An Australian name for the world during the time of Creation
echidna:	An Australian animal with sharp spines and a long, skinny snout
flowering wattle:	A name given by Australians to any acacia plant
kookaburra:	An Australian bird whose call sounds like laughter
wallaby grass:	A long-leafed plant that grows in Australia
wombat:	An Australian animal about the size of a badger

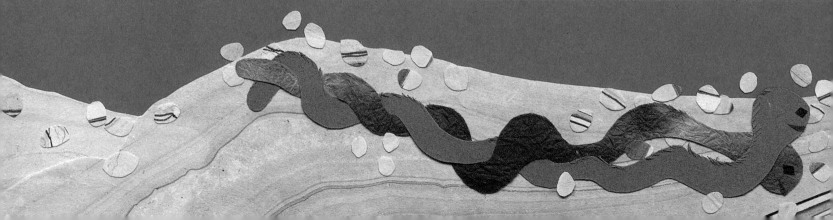